ODDITIES OF INTUITION

Alexander De Witte

Dormouse Publications

ODDITIES OF INTUITION

All poems by Alexander De Witte

except

<u>Punch Drunk</u> – Alexander De Witte and Stephen Pilling

and

<u>Down to the River</u> – Alexander De Witte and
Catching Creativity Project Participants

Copyright 2019 Alexander De Witte

All Rights Reserved

Cover design by Karen Lennox Williams

kazziedesigns@yahoo.com

For

Kevin Stamp
(colleague and creative mentor)

Introduction

To exist, incognito on the backs of old, used envelopes and on the tattered torn out pages of lined A4 writing pads, does not speak of any glory of poetic expression that most of us would deem fitting and noble. Yet over the course of twenty years, often misplaced and seemingly lost; in my estimation at least, this was my poetry's lot. This seems to me a fitting metaphor for all which is tenuous within both our creations and our waking moments generally. Once we ditch nostalgia and lofty sentiment we see that poetry is simply a part of life and everyone's poetry is different, just as our lives are distinct. Yet whatever the circumstance, our poetry reflects something about self. Moreover, when it spans a considerable period of time, its changes and shifts in style and emphasis paint a picture of not only specific moments within our experience, but also *how who we are becoming* has been born out of *who we have been*. Each time those poems were rediscovered, I vowed never to misplace them again, but invariably did. It is with relief I can say that finally the point of it all and the delays has become clear. Life is an adventure that we do not always journal. These fragments of me enable the pulling together of my sense of meaning and purpose. The layers of story we inhabit, are the very essence of our tenure on this planet. Here is a cross-section of the productive output of a twenty year span

The poems in this collection, of which there are sixty seven in total, reflect what have been three distinct phases within my poetic experience and expression. These phases have been given names, serving as sections of this collection. 1/ The Traditional 2/ The Mimetic and 3/ The Performative. They follow this order in the book, but chronologically, things went from traditional to performative and latterly into the mimetic. The mimetic section contains twenty one poems that were inspired by photographs, taken between October 2018 and February 2019, in a *rebuilding* phase of my life. I see mimesis as transmutation of essence into some other emanation of a thing, rather than the limiting notion of facsimile of some original phenomenon, which is then merely a copy; a replication lacking soul. Although my move toward performance poetry coincided with a work-based creativity project in 2011, I had my first encounter of what was to come, upon the death of my mother. I wrote a poem as an ode to my relationship to her and read it aloud at the funeral service. Already, in its construction, it became necessary to look more at the verbal impacts and their 'power to move' than the technical beauty and precision of some classical form. Looking back, this helps me see a connection between decay and reformulation – decay being the prerequisite for fertility's production of new forms. At that monumental rite of passage, a part of me died as well. But that poem (not that I could have known) was symbolic of my own forthcoming rebirth, through the performative.

Once I got established in the spoken word vein, I spent much of 2012 experimenting with both poetry in live settings and performance storytelling (the storytelling being more prominent until the end of 2015). Indeed, poetry appears to be simply *one form through which a story can be told.* Around 2012, there were still forays into traditional style, although it was becoming harder not to *hear the poetry being performed in my head* while attempting to write. Speech makes concessions to practicality, in terms of both content and communicability. The point is that a hearer is fundamentally different to a reader. So my forms of writing began gradually to collapse into one another. Even within my originally classical written-word bent (which had seen me experiment with some breakdown of forms and rejection, in dispatches, of rhyme – which for a time I found vulgar), there now came incursion of doggerel verse – simply because the point had become *impactful performance.*

At first I felt an inner resistance to these developments, but in the end I surrendered to its inevitability. This became a less bitter pill to swallow, once I had become familiar with Walter J. Ong's work <u>Orality and Literacy</u>. However, before arriving at Ong, and in order to rescue some semblance of classical order, I happened into the mimetic dimension by actively searching for new sources of inspiration from earlier poets. Upon reading Goethe's <u>New Love,</u>

New Life - and concerned about how his Romanticism was placing the *thrilling advent of new love* before the arrival of a new meaning to life – it struck me that copying his structure, it would be possible to invert his emphasis with a more 'true to life' account of love and the human condition. And so, I penned New Life, New Love two hundred and thirty years after Goethe produced his offering on the subject. This was my first experience of using something other than inward inspiration to oil the creative cogs. This little venture prepared the soil for me in recognising new sources of inspiration; albeit that I found it eventually more natural seeking poetic inspiration by exposure to a beautiful and/or otherwise stimulating photographic image. Thus was born a project I christened 'Beyond the Frame'. Even this latest phase of exploration, bears the hallmarks of the doggerel influences and the voice component necessary to engage a hearer, above the sensibilities for precision and eloquence found in a reader. As I edited and reviewed my selections it became clear that a fourth and final section 4/ Oddities would aptly reflect key transitional motifs within the three stages experienced on my poetic journey. I speak a little more about the four poems in that section within its brief introduction.

And now on my journey, I swing back to the performative and am currently exploring new dimensions of possibility. Thank you for choosing to look at this collection. My hope is that it will inspire you to be more avid with respect to your own creative niche and the contributions with which you may offer enrichment of soul, to your fellow travellers upon this spinning globe.

Alex Brocklehurst

April 2019

<u>Back Street By the Cemetery – Mytholmroyd.</u>

From Mytholmroyd to Haworth

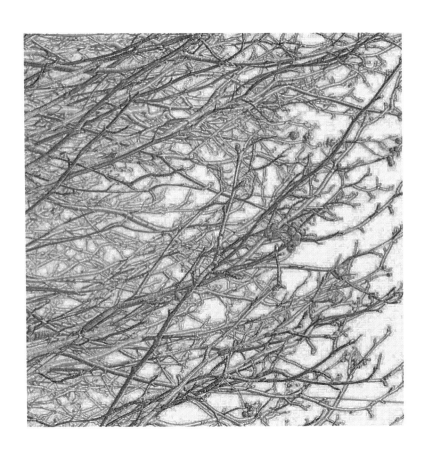

Fruiting Berries - Darwen

1. The Traditional

The Fire and the Rain

The fire and the rain
Driven against the skin… of time
Make no impression.
Awesome brutes, yet subtle;
Capturing something which cannot be imprisoned
and yet never able to vanquish
Since life is a shade, not a colour.

Come swim with me in the odour of life
Kindle your senses;
give up the fight.
Were they to run with me?
The world would stand still.
Whereupon all would discover,
the secret of the fire and the rain.

Birthing the Essence

Eternity sat in my breast
And sighed "How dearly I would love to blossom."
"Here and elsewhere, here and elsewhere."

It did not cajole, by way of noise
In no way presenting itself
It just sat there and cried.

Lonely, and in itself ignored
Unable to grow, in somebody else's clothes;
"Please meet with me" she cried,
"Or I shall die".

Discerning Spectre

Great words expressed
Great lives enfleshed
May, in a single second, perish.
Perhaps by recognition uncrowned
Perhaps by fire consumed.

And yet this ghost,
of all that never was;
Whose heartbeat forms
the echo of grief;
should not be feared
but instead embraced
For she alone mourns the passing
Of that architect of oblivion;
The fear-bound, sterile self.

Irregular Reflections

Irregular reflections
Cast no shadow
Feign no substance
Exhibit no glory

For something other to be there
than is seen
is ambivalent
enough to riddle
vanity or depth?
depth or vanity?
  For without remainder
  is there knowledge?
  from authorised wells alone
  to drink
  Is that absurd?

May the observer behold
May he drink his fill,
confidently
since his drinking
no other deprives,
and renders not its act
despised.

Heart of Strength

They were all great
  those young men
  those *other* men
  as they marched along the seashore.
They were not quite numberless
  although,
  it felt that way

Just then, a woman of years
Back crooked
Hair worn out
  Fragmented the horizon.
Stripping to undergarments
And improving of gait
she sprinted toward
inhospitable sea.
There she swam
  freely.
Riding rough waves,
  smiling.
Liberty
  so late
  in life, discovered
"I have always lived here"
She mouthed.

Sea of Inspiration

How great to wake
from slumber
with verse
The work of the muse
t'is never done
cogs of the imagination
simply rumble on.
Copyright?
not me
not me.

But may that virgin land remain
unsullied,
  not trodden underfoot.
  May alien senses satiate
  merely to return with gifts,
  Not harbouring plans
  to domesticate
  nor ameliorate
  nor infiltrate;
  but to preserve.

Cycles not Circles

What life once was
t'will never again be
the image of the parents
in the children we see
unquestionably similar
yet not the same
a snapshot of life
in a different frame.

Although to look forward
might banish regret
time still marches onward
giving occasion to fret.
For identical or different
t'is all the same
each merely plays a variation
of a time-honoured game.
When all said and done
At the end of our lease
t'is another that shall read
'here lies,
 aged,
 rest in peace.'

Crossroads

O ne'er forgotten friend
would time or tide pretend?
  or hasten such decay
  that one lack not the will
  but the means?

Though slumber little change dictates
t'is here no beast that hibernates
  and once th'inclement time is past
  rolling landscape portends of something new
What shall the herald be?
Or shall winter abide, eternally?

Dislocated Consciousness

Evening past
sleep eludes
the hunted man,
but not the world.
Of troubled mind
in body weary
  rest escapes perpetually.
  One eye open, spies the feline
  One eye open, the gaze returned,
  then the whispering voice of wisdom,
  in but an instant, life lesson learned.
Settle not for shadows, child,
that precious seconds be not spurned.
Rather let the senses spin
to release at last, the fire within.

Are the Mourners Comforted?

How long O LORD? The prophets did cry
That cry no more, should my spirit die

For with me it seems, their whole number dwell
A burden of imprisoning pain to me, as hell

A legion of the sorely oppressed righteous, birthed
O what be this mystery within me unearthed?

I bear it not well, nails driving deep
As agony, with suffusion into my soul, doth creep

And numberless, faceless victims weep
Their inconsolable wail of grief so deep

Those untouched, continue in their slumber
Their dreams satiated with goods beyond number

Yet with this morsel my heart I console
That life's burden is lighter when etched in my soul

From whence, O LORD, shall my respite come?
Since t'is here on Earth I must make my home

…despite your setting eternity in the hearts of men
That they discover not what comes after them

And so, LORD, will the mourners be comforted?
Or is it their lot to be endlessly buffeted?

In fathomless depths, life's lessons learned, spirits lift
A community of hearts, depth of pain, felt as gift

Alas O LORD, How long shall my comfort tarry?
"O true disciple of mine, who truly lives. What's the hurry?"

Emergence Celebration

Lingering winter, no flower would grow
Dwelling so long and deep
Hardened earth and desolate cry
Barren. Not even solitude
Alas, no fortitude.
Meanwhile something stirred
Imperceptible to human eye
Small creatures noticed first
And the insects began to play
Soon to flourish against the grain
Life again, will have its way
The most beautiful flower emerged...
Putting the landscape to shame
"I've been hiding..."
It cried
The Earth wept for joy
Breathed deeply once more...
and gathered the strength to dance with the stars.

Changeling

My pain is maturing, growing up
No more an ingrowing nail, acutely felt

Danger past of a septic turn
Its containment shows me how truly to feel

Neither are you arthritic in flavour
Gnarling me up, in bitterness, twisted

More akin to blisters on the feet
With moments of rest, the respite is sweet

Inspiration comes in multiple shades
As ambivalence percolates my soul
Effervescences, which unlike oil and water, mix
Two disparate visions somehow embrace, then desist

And this leaves me where, my nomadic spirit?
Waiting, pondering, anticipating the dawn

Still, now I know my one and only home,
t'is in my heart and there alone.

Gem

Pure, unsoiled, untainted
Portrait of eternal moment, born in you
An innocence which makes the heart sing.

Battered, bruised, worn down
Through changing landscapes of life, longing
A burden which darkens the soul.

Parched, famished, weakened
Overwhelming journey, seeking essence of joy
A nightmare seemingly chases all hope away.

Reviving, renewing, reborn – in time
Effervescence of perfect beauty emerges
Triumphant, enduring courage shapes the sapphire that is you.

Epic Flight

Still
Heart beating, heart weeping
Spirit feeling, life reaching
Bird soaring, far above the clouds

I rise
To meet Thee, glide with me
Entwined and made free, by life's decree
Morning Sun, soon will light the skies

Further
We stretch, as to horizons aspiring
The moments of calm, assuage the tiring
Where can we travel, my heart?

Aching
With longing, distracted in pondering
Shall you tarry with me, that I might fulfil thee?
For the journey is the goal
Wherever we may go

Stained Glass Illusion

You to me were stained glass window
Untouchable, out of reach, remote.

Would that I could have joined you there
More likely than that you joined me here

Delusions of a mind's wishful thinking
Condemned forever a realist to be

Wrestling, all the while dreams crippled
Writhing bereft, amid human debris

Why oh why? Protests my soul
Does exquisite torture my portion remain?

Your breath misted the air, pulse cadent beneath your skin
Yet no entwining hearts, beat here as one

Alas shall such a moment ever be...
When any outside that window I touch, taste or even see?

An Agitation Transformation

Embracing the gentle breeze
Senses whipped up as autumn leaves

Surveying life's subtleties from the edges
Wonders within my soul converge as privileges

Were you to walk, as upon clouds
Mystery, not curiosity, your heart would rouse

And fire within your spirit would rise
As dreams soar upward toward bluer skies

As one, enlightened congregation to life's highest aspires
Whilst all that blights, against such movement conspires

And hordes rampage, trampling underfoot
Alas… connections with worlds of vanity must be cut

My invitation you receive, to sing from our hearts
From whence, corruption of transforming love shall depart.

Essence

Echoing to you from deep and mysterious place
Oceans, whirlpools, waterfalls speak not of power, but beauty
Emergent as from chrysalis, is born serenity.

Passionate torrents rage, yet subside
Assuaged, the deafened notice not the ebb of the tide
its gentle, lapping murmur whispers "forget me not".

Awake or in dreams, a deeper shade to surface
In volcanic eruption, containing both more and less of you
Giving and being replenished… a sigh felt; released.

Sensing the pain of labour, irreversible moment ever near
Tantalising taste of sweet anticipation, comforts
Vistas of new possibility on horizons appear.

Myriad shades of virtue, dwell not in man-made cage
But, as when birds released, begin in formation to fly
Such will be the spirit of you; heart soaring, being true.

The Mystic's Fall From Grace

I cannot bear to soil Thee
Thou art so pristine and pure
Yet lofty, may seem out of reach
as the heart beats in a conflict – bitter sweet.

Ache, sigh, cry. This leaden heart of mine
Break out, break free. The spiralling path before me.
High brought low and low lifted high
Shall this raging torrent, my reservations belie?

Oh icon, tenderly reposing in my heart
Shall it be that we make a fresh start?
Or will the day darken and fade
and Sun set forever, on all that together… we made?

Written in 'emotional' blood…
My love.

Moment

Sat on a bench
Beneath a sprawling bush
Or is it a tree?
I only know it is sheltering me.

Dancing in the breeze
Twig and leaf gently kiss
Again and once more
Tenderness to make the spirit soar

A parable of love
Cradle of divine protection?
Eternity captured in a moment
Left behind, a sense of torment

When shall I move on?
Return to the grind
Surely I cannot linger here?
Perhaps I'll shed the moment as a tear

A dilemma. Remain or be rushed?
Important things clamour and call
What then, is my decision to be?
I'm taking the moment with me.

The Truth, She is Lived

Standing, bending, squinting;
through net curtain they peer in
A macabre bunch queue,
for a glimpse of your 'sin'
Wide, small, tall, round or thin
You feel them whispering –
but they don't live within
(your skin)
What would they know; those idle spectators?
Those malcontent voyeurs;
turned moralistic dictators
And so, shall your response be
compassion or contempt?
Since from humanity,
it must be said,
they make themselves exempt
Stand up, stand at full height –
venture forth from there
Breathe fresh air into your nostrils –
choose life, without any fear
Next, select your scenery;
it transforms with you, as you move
At last, release discovered;
through life lived in its groove
Then, upon finding your rhythm,
with anticipation you'll look around
Observing that the expectations of miscreants,
no longer can be found
And you'll sense in the glee,
of long overdue liberty
T'is those left behind who are bound.

Paradise

Morning Sun broke into a smile, through the clouds
Hair ruffled in the breeze, lungs filling deep
The spirit of life danced within.
The bird singing its melodic tune, reminds me
Of an ancient song
One without words
...which broods and stirs
The heart lifts up
This moment is a portrait of me, of life, of joy
The mind intrudes presently; is there a thing amiss?
Battle temporarily rages, among the soldiers arrayed within
Missing; what could be missing?
Simply because I do not notice, does that mean I do not care?
Seemingly, transfigured in this moment, senses had been misplaced
Glancing sideways, suddenly all becomes crystal clear
That which was missing was you.
I'd felt complete, while being unaware of you. How so?
Still, you had been there,
holding my hand as we traversed the shore
Our eyes meeting, we spoke without words
Your eyes told me you had felt complete too
Yet hardly aware I was there
We sat down and with our fingers, drew figures in the sand
And we knew that true comfort had been found.

Merging

It really didn't matter
I'd been many times before
Wonderful contours
Angled shapes galore
Some parts more spacious
Others you just squeezed in
Though dark, never barren
Never unwelcoming, or dry
A gentle stream it trickles
guiding me while I pry
An experience of wild adventure
Inspiring so much as to cry
Offering such exquisite satisfaction
Moving the soul to sigh
Each time I come it's different
Yet, whichever way
renders me content
Each adventure leaves me breathless
Bringing fulfilment,
not duress
Oh the journey here,
is where the journey must begin
For the interior of this cavern
reflects the one that is within
In exploring it,
I am exploring me
It is a lost and ancient way
to experience being free
As the path unfolds
Forever in readiness

To be tantalised by exchanges
toward spiritual headiness
And to tarry with you there,
in that sacred place we share.

The Darkness of the Light

Some call it the Dark Night of the Soul
when your passage to becoming whole
invites a vortex from some otherworldly realm
to open, in the ground, all around you.

Each tentative step your own
a journey of lifetimes unknown
springs forth to make your head spin
and it feels that your respite is distant.

Do not be forlorn my love
for peace shall wing its way to you as a dove
and as you stretch your hand out in the dark
your fingertips touch mine and tell you…

You are not alone, though in distress
as your well of tears flows to excess
and although the pain must do its task
dawn is soon born, on the horizon.

Hold tightly to your aching heart
for in that space your future will start
and you as butterfly shall appear
whose elegance and finery shall be; the essence…

of your reborn, magnificent spirit.

Within is Without

Movement, intense, deep, earth-shattering
What profound mystery stirs here?
Avenues open up in the soul
Furrows ploughed, through awakened spirit
Connected, imbued, drenched – with awe
Born from strangely dormant place
Then, strides out into 'that which is'
Celebrates length, depth, breadth of a beautiful ocean
...called Life.

Voyaging, directed, exploring, discovering
Deepest revelation lies where?
Passion awakens in the heart
Energy thrown off, through coursing veins
Aching, yearning, driven – with longing
Maturing from restless, chaotic place
Then, moves out tenaciously in faith
Embraces creativity, purpose, power of a torrid storm
...called Living.

The Crimson Goat

Lo, he is tethered,
the Crimson Goat,
to yonder lonely silver birch
With cord so fine,
that one would think,
to chafe it,
would quickly snap
..that which binds.
At the first he pulled;
next he strained
and then shook,
alas to no avail.
And so, resigned,
he consumed the grass;
all around his fleet hooves
and unto the restraining cord's
full extent.
Until through time,
no lush verdant grass,
there remained
and even this hardy mountain creature,
no more could muster smile.
And when, deprived of nourishment
that body requires,
emaciation beckoned
and he physically pined;
so, he sat and pondered and mused,
until he knew himself,
like none that freedom first did choose:
A carcass now,

yet remaining alive..
As Tantalus for a time he lived,
as his beard lengthened,
coarse and strong,
his underbelly soiled,
discoloured from barren earth;
until finally he longed,
enough for that
which lay beyond..
And so, with last ounce of resolve, did he
finally chew through
that imprisoning cord
and with lingering dregs of life force;
wearily sauntered into that place..
where at last his portion
was not simply to survive,
Rather thrive.

Chariots

Daylight long since grown faint
In a space of eerie, elusive shadow
As the west wind gently blows
Under shelter of magic willow
The nomadic ones repose, content.

A nightingale's soulful melody
Conduit to an otherworldly realm
Wherein all memory of return, ere long
Into vicissitudes of inexorable fate, is lost.

Reciting a lyric, deeply inspired
From heartbeat of the ancient lyre
Sacred dance will serenely transport
To a beyond which is Persephone's home
Harboured safe by Hermes' wand

Yea by Caduceus charm transcend the mortal veil
That, fleetingly, pilgrim paths should merge
In soil the ancients trod
And with timeless erudition return

Enchantment borne upon nocturnal breeze
As lemon-tinged tonic, in chariots of moon-vine scent
What alchemy this, that revivifies the soul
As the water nymph, in garb of magic hue
Rides the reflected moon's watery haze?

She hovers at horizon where earth and waters meet
Then, upon lagoon's surface, glides

To bequeath to the land, her morning dew
Dew, like mortal flesh
Replenished with reservoirs of resolve

Yea, Cosmic Charger, ride to destiny's plight
And so, upon rolling back the canopy of the night
Plead once more, that the role adopt the man
- As sacred custodian toward all that brings life.

New Life, New Love

Fear, why do you not ensnare anymore?
Controlling neither me nor mine
Relaxed, a novelty not seen before
As when Christ turned water into wine
Grief has abandoned the stomach's pit
Intellectual masturbation over, I reach for the experiential clit
Sweet release of a different hue
Was this not long overdue?

Within a lover's beauty shall danger lurk?
Distracting from the pressing task
Luring from the reinventing work
All pretence, necessity now unmasks
Still, mighty Rome was not built in a day
Neither time nor tide could halt its decay
As to breathe is to be imperfect
So life emerges in every defect.

What force this? Levelling me with her eyes
Like midsummer Sun, as it streams from the skies
Radiant intensity lays me instantly bare
Telling my very bones, I truly care
Then arrives illumination in my soul
At last, all the parts fashion a satisfying whole
And the point of it all is clearly seen.

2. The Mimetic

Gateway

Portal. Conduit for this mortal.
The invitation alluring,
wonderment procuring.
How to be in two spaces at once…
in a cosmic resonance.
The swell of inspiration,
a transformation emanation.
Oh, to stretch toward horizons new
in such a zone, where doubts are few.
No longer passive but passionate;
enlivened soul can relate...
to this burning flame
that feels propelled,
beyond the frame...

Matter Over Mind

Permanence and transience,
transport to realms of prescience.
You see the retinal image,
before your senses can finish…
noting all that is there.
You start some place
and end up elsewhere.
Are your choices truly felt, in your heart?
Or is your body merely dragged along
in another person's cart?
It's time to begin,
searching within
for the true lens
with which you may make amends…
for all the old fudges
and the long held grudges…
which blunted your soul.
You have it all to gain
when you leap into the scene
beyond the frame…

Simulation the Curse

Contours and detours and journeys and scenes –
panoramas and visions and inspiring themes.
Our brains take a snapshot of each moment in time –
it passes and yet may be captured in rhyme.
Every second contains the essence of freedom,
the chance to be undisputed lord of one's fiefdom.
Life passes so fast that often we fail to pause…
so as to invoke that vital clause...
that says "no longer feign, life beyond the frame"

The Mouth's Money

A story of dreams, ripped at the seams
unless you possess the means to step outside the routines.
Contrast comes at a price, where sentiment will not suffice.
A picture painting myriad words,
like the face that launched a thousand ships,
to bring something beautiful home - that inspired an epic tome
of life lived not in the fast lane;
rather savoured, beyond the frame...

Coming Home to Oneself

Today, the day
you stop reaching
for illusion,
the old you
now drawn
into dissolution.

Reaching for
the mirage
no longer,
you sense
a refreshing
sort of hunger
for that
which is real –
it is visceral;
can you feel?

Reinventing
the misshapen wheel
no more,
expect joyous
experiences galore..
which long awaited
this change of tack,
from which
there is
no going back.

You will not
enter free fall.
Instead you can
have it all…
with a leap not of faith,
but trust.
What you reach for
will not
rust.

For it is grounded,
well rounded
and certainly founded
on attributes that are...
solid.

Things shall
no longer
remain inane.
Reach now
for life
...beyond the frame.

Temptation, Beyond Fear of Damnation

An invitation,
worry or anticipation?
Ghosts may trap you there,
should you venture within –
will you find a home,
or some evil gnome,
offering retribution
for all you've never done?
Exercising choice is the discovery
of your true voice;
the one which says "I am free",
not constrained in demonic glee,
by those who direct your path…
to a life of wrath,
at opportunities wasted…
of delights never tasted.
It's time to stake your claim,
upon a richer experience
beyond the frame.

Ghost Architect

Ruined, dishevelled - civilisation levelled.
Curiosity toward a bygone time,
as dilapidation supersedes the sublime.
Angles yet exist, despite structures that desist.
No need to excavate or renovate, nor even ameliorate.
Order still may subtly prevail,
even where human endeavour may fail.
History bleeds, an epoch recedes…
life trundles on, though the embodiment is gone.
And so, through every lens, decay may make amends;
with this human game
that strives for life... beyond the frame.

Invitation to the Next Station

Colours and textures abundant –
the need for melancholy redundant.
Curiosity sparked, boredom parked..
images clamour, which transcend shallow glamour.
Inspiration seeks its next story, beauty is the true glory...
that elevates the soul.
Finding joy in simplicity, provides the spiritual electricity,
to light up your life.. once mundanity becomes rife.
Nature heard loudly to proclaim that "more lies in wait"
beyond the frame.

Magic, Within the In-Between

Sky's the limit - reflected in how you feel
oh how the layers peel
..back.
Perhaps one can have it all;
perchance pride comes before a fall.
Yet within this scene,
where brown and gold have replaced green –
the truth can readily be seen.
Horizons everywhere,
liminality inviting you to dare.
Do you even care?
Hiding away… shall never win the day.
Colourful must be balanced with grey…
stick or twist the game you play.
You see, success is rarely about fame –
but is forever born in communion [with possibilities]
beyond the frame.

Threshold

Portals and conduits, there they are.
We pass through without a sense of all that's new.. and magic;
dispelling all that was tragic.
Feeling alive is the freedom to thrive,
with a sense of abundance that isn't all down to you.
Can't you feel that is true?
What is noticed is the routine and familiar,
the structures which uphold the pronouncements of the conciliar.
No longer for me, the feeling of unfree.
Overturn the profane, transcend the mundane
and transition into new joys beyond the frame.

Corpus Callosum

Facsimile - in close proximity.
The eye deceives, the brain receives, signals...
hemispherically, realistically.
Yet, fact or imagination
which is real and which an aberration?
What *is*, projected onto a screen.
Still.. what *is*, may never have been...
When illusion is your delusion,
time beckons toward the fusion
of dream.. and what may be truly seen,
once one discards every filter
those longings that throw one out of kilter.
Your prison cell opens wide
and you begin to turn the tide;
once you notice that identical is not the same...
and in clarity you rise to meet life,
beyond the frame

Resolve

The future is murky, clouded, obscure –
it's there, yet still you can't be sure;
if what you were told, so eloquently sold,
by the purveyors of faith.. is really safe.
When you catch a glimpse and you wonder if this is rinse…
and repeat;
remind yourself that the edges are rarely neat.
If you feel rejected, if you've been deselected,
remember the only way out is through –
on the journey back to you.
Rest here a while, rediscover your unique style, in the peaceful isle…
of nature: before re-igniting your flame,
beyond the frame...

Dross

Surely that which is discarded is not regarded...
for its beauty?
Dead, useless, gone - its value is none, nil ,zero –
you are yesterday's hero...
and tomorrow's mulch.
Cut off from vitality's source,
the difference between death and life
may augur strife;
yet "where hither now?" becomes the inexorable vow..
of the searching soul, questing again to be whole.
The way isn't 'here', nor is it paralysis in fear,
or entrapment within a tear.
For death cannot tame
life beyond the frame.

Sensate Focus

There's an oasis 'out there' they tell me –
if you can just persevere enough to locate it.
And well, what you give your attention to,
will define the outcome due.
A jungle, a thicket, never mind that you didn't pick it.
There are worlds within worlds and adventures to unfurl,
when the courage of explorers you adorn…
and jettison all that is forlorn.
Venture on, venture through.
Rest awhile, enjoy the view.
Remember, once you confront the pain…
that *feeling* is entry into vitality,
beyond the frame.

Beneath the Truth

How many ways to turn yourself inside out –
scream, cry, shout...
When left is right and right is left and your aching soul feels bereft;
recall the focus, both remember and forget the detail.
Broad brush strokes remind,
that joy you can once again find,
in texture and tone - rather than milking the stone..
for detail.. which is merely a snare.
Lament not what is lost, nor its imagined cost;
but celebrate the spark within you, the living flame –
weaving anew your story
beyond the frame.

Follow the Rainbow

Expansive trails of light and colour,
make the humdrum often faced,
even duller.
One cannot simply order an iridescent day
like some hors d'oeuvre served on a tray.
What leads you to transcendence
...is half choice, half chance
much like your prospects when contemplating romance.
Yet, once your soul is inspired, you ache to meet the day –
unlike the opposite
when all seems grey.
You can curse, you can blame,
or you can follow the rainbow...
beyond the frame.

The Glorious Now

Permanence, a monument of yesterday –
a seismic shift might redesign the way... ahead.
Chaos unwanted may birth cataclysm
we may nonetheless face, undaunted.
Something made pristine begins immediately to slide into memory.
Make it live again!
Inscribe a message on petrified stone...
that you imagined within yesterday you could make your home.
You see, it all fades, just like fame.
It's time to embrace fresh synergies... beyond the frame.

Borderland

Is beauty to be found in symmetry, or cacophony, or both?
Is regimentation or wildness the measure of growth?
Two worlds may at times collide, in the space where desire meets pride.
A boundary may for a moment exist, then desist.
And where then will you position yourself?
Harmony is some kind of Holy Grail,
but when does it become an epic fail?
When all the parts fit but the heart is missing,
we enter the twilight of reminiscing.
You had it good once... when you weren't obsessed with taming.
Don't impose on experience some familiar name.
Embrace the "Je ne sais quoi" beyond the frame.

Return to Source

Tenacity in the teeth of vibrancy.
Of all the things to inspire the soul,
awe brought forth from diamonds, or the latency of coal;
the 'common' undergirds the rare;
the overlooked screams above the fanfare –
the rush, the clamour to be transported into a vision,
shows the subtle beauty of those objects destined for derision...
and decay.
Alas, may we all learn to appreciate the ephemeral some day –
and the tear which leaks from the corner of the eye,
unnoticed by most, but which poignancy lifts high.

T'is both noble and wise to perceive beauty
...beyond the Frame.

Holy Impetus

Adornment as refinement, the eye appreciates alignment,
while the river rolls.. green and grey unfolds and beauty cajoles,
with its siren song - to follow a route;
to be enticed, into a land outside this zeitgeist.
It's a matter of perspective, you see - this elixir called 'being free'.
It's time to notice, it's time to vote 'yes',
to a vantage point that has surrendered being lame –
instead boldly striding.. toward life,
beyond the frame.

Follow the Light

The Sun opposes the waters.
Death soon, so soon, makes way for life and her daughters.
The way of surrender has no ulterior agenda.
Time to let go, time to roll with the flow
and cease your resisting –
now is the end of persisting.
Release it all and like each brown leaf that did fall,
accept your fate - it's never too late;
to renounce your pain...
and accept the unknown,
beckoning...
beyond the frame.

3. The Performative

Ineffable Elixir

What is it to feel, happy..
to be happy.. to live happy?
One's meat is another's poison,
So they say
Quintessential happiness,
show me the way.
An endless quest for novelty,
or contentment with my lot?
Should happiness become my obsession
So I finally lose the plot?
In simplicity or complexity
Shall this elusive elixir be found?
Were I a master alchemist
Others happiness might I confound?
Happiness then, is everywhere
And nowhere at the same time
Both a mole hill and a mountain
For each of us to climb.
So what, for me, is happiness;
The unique vision to dispel doom?
T'is eminently the creative moment
Whence flower from bud
…doth bloom.

Releasing the Victim

They say that demons may possess you
That other people's control will certainly depress you
While overpowering circumstance will surely distress you
Alas, a single person makes the heart true
… and that is you
Stepping out to embrace the grind
Via open heart, your soul you'll find
A connection with life, leaving alienation behind
Take down your protective 'No Entry' sign
Life's efforts to change you, no longer malign
Above all, live in your body not in your mind
Feel the yearning, the burning desire
Like phoenix rise up from your past's funeral pyre
No longer to wallow in obsession's taxing mire
Free at last to live in the moment
No longer enslaved to a life so dormant
Anticipation born of possibilities rampant
Aligning with that which makes the heart sing
Birthing in the soul all that happiness would bring
Over time and destiny thy spirit will be king
You can have a clean slate
So step up to the plate
… and demons or not, embrace your fate.

What is Dark?

The callous night, it ate my heart
As the New Moon offered its fresh start
I'd never truly understood the part
that the ogre in the shadows played.

Adeptly I surfed upon quicksilver clouds
My heart in repose 'neath a maudlin shroud
Not once daring to shriek aloud
as the wolf o'er my soul it bayed.

Once the walls came crashing down
The ogre unmasked itself within my frown
And pondering, I felt myself a clown
whose disguise my bleeding heart had betrayed.

The callous night it, ate my heart
Yet as the New Moon offered its fresh start
My choice to let illusions depart
Freed my captive soul from dismay.

The Gentle Call of the Distant Mists

Staring at the empty chair where you should be
Eternity is captured in a moment, then set free
And so, what do we see?

I awoke to find myself in a dream
You were there mum, young and pristine
And as you walked through a sun-drenched meadow
You were healthy once more
Vitality coursed through your veins, your heart, your very soul

I saw all the possibilities for your earthly life
That you gave up for me in maternal sacrifice
And I saw, as if for the first time, the depth of your love
Yet still you would smile and nod and say
"I would have it no other way"

And although time has halted its earthly motion
The river shall never flow backwards to the ocean
Though the Sun long since shone its rays onto your mortal flesh
The gentleness of autumn has prepared for the winter of the soul
- before the spring comes again

Hand in hand we came to a beautiful silver tree
Short yet elegant, swaying regally in the breeze
It stood out like an elder monarch
Whose grey hair tells of wisdom, honour and high regard
Speaking without words, of eternal truths – that should never be forsaken
In the world between worlds we glimpse perpetual rest
- and in a moment everything is seen and felt

Now, as you leave my side and smile
You cross the bridge into the ancient mountain mists
I see you turn, wave and blow me a kiss
Before you continue your journey into the beyond
And the love you leave behind, shall dwell in my heart as our bond.
Au revoir my love.

Spring

I am spring's awakening scenes and gentle warmth

I am nature's newest brushstroke of colour in many a month

I am the scent of wild garlic and odours of light, musty earth

I am the resplendent cherry blossom that speaks of nuptials and birth

I am amorous ducks that quack and geese that hoot

I am the freshly budding tree, ready to acquire his new suit

I am like the dawn within the cycle of a single day

…and the morning of a life; as innocence and wonder begin to play

I am the shift you see when ants invade your kitchen

I am Houdini escaping winter's chains in time for ditching

Summer

I am summer's glittering Sun and cloudless skies

I am iridescent wings of dancing butterflies

I am the ripening fruit upon the expectant tree

I am the mesmeric dance of the pollinating bee

I am the lengthening day and the receding night

I am the fledgling bird making her maiden flight

I am like the noon within the cycle of a single day

…and the Sun's zenith within a life; before the advent of decay

I am the holiday season, where faith and joy abide

I am herald of autumn's bounty, from vitality supplied

Autumn

I am autumn's moody skies and dampening chills

I am yellow and brown foliage becoming green at the gills

I am that first intrepid leaf to take to the air

I am the sharp whip of wind that races through your hair

I am the woodland toadstool clinging wearily to life

I am the scurrying squirrel hoarding bounty for winter's strife

I am like the evening within the cycle of a single day

...and the twilight of a life; as the hair tints with grey

I am the mature pine cone, freshly fallen from the tree

I am the spirit of sparkling summer sunsets, set free

Winter

I am winter's darkened nights and icy winds

I am the ghostly birch that haunts with outstretched limbs

I am the frozen lake upon which graceful swans trundle

I am the vibrant orange breast of the robin that remains forever humble

I am the barren landscape where tranquil beauty is heard in echo

I am the footprint of every creature ever to grace the snow

I am like the night within the cycle of a single day

…and the midnight of a life; as sands of time slip away

I am the hibernation phase, where fears and gremlins lurk

I am the midwife of spring's new birth, set patiently to work

Outside In

Twisted roots, upturned bereft **(4)**
A memorial to conflict, laid bare **(6)**
The pecan tree, so wantonly hacked down **(7)**
Despite surviving the withering drought **(5)**

Sweet agony lies there
Joyful to have existed at all
Our mortally wounded friend now softly sings
The primaeval ballad of life

Rhythmic echoes I hear
The pulsing of an ancient drum
Trance carries me up, way up above
Beyond soothing, emerald-tinged stars

Pebbly River, Milky Way
The Holy Ganges of the sky
Comets in spiral arms, with rainbows arrayed
Illuminating mists of ebbing time

Pinks, blues, oranges, mauves
Iridescent clouds of light and life
Mesmerise before I turn and serenely traverse
Caverns of dark, eternal span

In pirouette, Andromeda encircled
Beyond and then within, I wheel
The Jewel Box; The Butterfly; The Beehive
Draw me to Orion's embrace

Journeying back momentously back
Neptune, Uranus, Saturn, Jupiter I see
Before Mars rampaging roars raucously "Moon ahoy!"
Still her path unfolds delicately

Blink of hawk's eye
To glide over both snowy poles
Oceans, islands, streams – mountains and volcanoes scaled
Until at last, I return
Pecan leaf quickly spied
Enter I into one fragile vein
Alchemy beyond comprehension – renders mystical union complete
Through rhythmic drum beat... announced

Flesh and sinews welded
Dark yet warm, strange yet familiar
A sudden rush, a strange new world
I take my first breath.

Crossing that Line

Why are you here?
Why am I here?
Why are we here?
For inspiration or fear?

Shall we create life?
Shall we manufacture strife?
Or shall we balance on that knife?
Churning with inspiration and fear.

Will you see me in the end?
Turning left, then right, do you see a friend?
Are our aching hearts truly on the mend?
Celebrating inspiration; displacing fear.

Could you step up to the plate?
…Contemplate creating your own fate?
Is it really too late?
…to choose inspiration over fear.

Is it safe to watch from the wings?
…To be rooted to my seat while my spirit sings?
…To swim around numb, in a world full of things?
Neglecting inspiration in favour of fear.

Why are you here?
Why am I here?
Why are we here?
For inspiration or fear?

The Essence of War

So, what IS war – except victory and defeat?
Do the hearts of those who wage it ever truly meet?
Curious it is that it always happens 'out there'.
…On some cold frontier, where enemies lurk in some lair.

Whether a moral crusade or perchance a Holy War,
Can any deny they have seen it all before?
Are the pawns in this game vicious wolves or lambs to the slaughter?
Will we find answers upon the face of a bereaved wife or daughter?

Do the good die young and the bad die old?
It all depends by whom the story is told.
Is it truly glory and honour that fights 'til the last breath?
Or is the fate of each casualty simply an unsavoury death?

A glint of steel, piercing cold and grey.
Frames a picture seen on many a day
Whether of a bayonet by which another is thrust through
Or the killer's eyes, a person just like you.

Whether philosopher, poet, priest or king
What timeless truth might any spectator bring?
To the endless stories about torrents of wailing blood
That screams from the earth that men's hearts are not good…

So gallant friends, might I ask you to decide
As you consider the life that to your left and right resides
Whether friend or foe, stranger or lover; what might they do?
Should you wage war and cut them, would they not bleed
…just like you?

Race

Walking, running, panting, breathing
Lungs which burst, a burning feeling
This race, I face, at pace, is a disgrace...
Slowly, torturously, killing me
When will I be free?
Looking left, then looking right
Strange adrenaline this – fright or delight?
Maybe I need it and it needs me too
A partnership of necessity, stronger than glue
Leave it behind, liberate your mind...
...that little voice which says "I can't, I must, I should,"
Burn it down now, it's all dead wood

...If only I could.

Time nor Tide

One year ago today, I departed the fray

You never know what's going to change –

what life might soon rearrange

In politics or love, will you face a hawk

… or a dove?

You've only got your own perspective

But that view is not reflective, it's selective

You see, you've got to make things happen

Cos life's not a fashion

… parade

It's not pink lemonade

or unicorns

- you bleed when stabbed by thorns

You've got to reach for your goals

You have to be bold. You see this story is old

Whether or not it's been endlessly retold

That old game, called blame

won't bequeath you any fame. No… blame…

… is just lame

Brothers and sisters, when your feet earn their blisters

life opens up to you new vistas

There's nothing certain, no guarantees

no indemnity, you don't get to charge fees

And when life brings you to your knees…

remember this:

The highest rewards are not earned in bliss –

but in the heart of the abyss

You are not a victim in need of protection

You're a winner saying no to de-selection

It's not enough to have dreams...

Success is not located in hare-brained schemes

Inside you there is a voice – the author of every choice...

you'll ever make – to not be fake

It's like a candle flame, transforming into raging fire

... by your own desire – by your determination to be heard,

not to finish second or third

but to prevail in the race with yourself – not to sit on some isolated shelf

Discover your passion and live

Dedicate your achievements to all who never did...

... but who ran the other way and hid

One year ago today, I departed the fray

You never know what's going to change

except...

You

Bowels of Decay

Reducing life to a solitary dimension
Harbouring not one ounce of pretension
toward celebration of anything exemplary
Instead seeking to assimilate
With those who merely imitate
The schemes that garner profit
You see, it's not just popular culture
…which attracts the profiteering vulture
For even that which is lofty… commands its price.

It's got to be said, as I lift my hands to my forehead
That there is no shock at the streaks of red
You see, both hands bled
Now, this may not be evidence of the stigmata
But this truth which bleeds is more ancient than the Magna Carta

Or Christ…

Whether the left hand or the right
Classical and popular have been torn in the same fight
You might think mass culture has always been flawed
…and wonder why the higher forms got 'outlawed'
Newsflash: Truth in-coming…
Classical culture got lynched – it was hijacked
Aesthetic sensibilities got unceremoniously whacked
…by ideological mafia running their racket
…dressed up like a lord in his tweed jacket
And because "man shall not live by bread alone"
the cannibals have stripped our flesh to the bone
And so, from the body, the spirit has flown

Now the gullible continue to be led – as flesh above soul is fed
So many now believe all that they are told… (and once challenged)
…bestow upon you tin-foil hat, rather than crown of gold
When those bleeding, agonised hands reach out,
As if miming an ancient voice…
It's no political slogan, it's no ideological tack
when the blood shall roar…
"It's time to take our culture back."

Prescriptive Vision in Derision

Our Father who art in heaven
The orthodoxy taught before turning seven
Not so much a prayer as a script
Like life's mummification, destined for the crypt
Hallowed be Thy Name
Now it's clear who is to blame
For every measure by which we fall short
For each self-doubt we ever bought
Thy Kingdom Come, Thy Will be done
Convent or monastery, neither much fun
For those who would be upright, not uptight
When out of the cosmic overlord's sight
On Earth as it is in heaven
See now, this is relevant, cos I just turned eleven
Knowing what defines the straight and narrow
Leads to the main stage, not the side show
Give us this day our daily bread
A mantra for the crack house, when not being fed
There's many who'd be happy to replace God with the state
But they should remember food banks, when so many haven't ate
And forgive us our trespasses
Might just be the wrong emphasis
When the disenfranchised have no stability
Because of the law givers' lack of reliability
As we forgive those who trespass against us
You're kidding right? Forgiveness grants no buzz
Especially on a one way street
When your nemesis keeps turning up the heat
And lead us not into temptation
Speak for yourself; I'm up for the invitation

To test the very essence of my mettle

Because with weakness you should never settle

But deliver us from evil

Well.. evil is truly primaeval

So if I can escape it every single time

Perhaps I'll give you thanks and end this rhyme

For Thine is the Kingdom, the power and the glory

I'm starting to question my place in this story

You see, I'm looking for a bit of meaningful autonomy

How much space is there for me in this divine homily?

For ever and ever

So there's no ending to it whatsoever?

I don't know if that's something folk should mandate

Or the kind of theocracy they should seek to abrogate

Amen.

Time to reprise it again…

4. Oddities

Summation

This fourth section serves as a postscript for the collection. I played with creating new forms through mimesis. I bounced off Johann Wolfgang von Goethe but settled on using strong visuals as my preferred method for seeking new inspiration (rather than the literary). I played around in <u>Outside In</u> with other new 'styles' - not quite Haiku or Acrostic, but repeating in this case 4,6,7,5 words in each line in sequence for each unfolding stanza – within a performative rather than literary piece.

I have arrived at my notion of 'storied verse' and the story which emerges behind the details of twists and shifts of emphasis is told best I feel, via the twin concepts of decay and re-emergence. Two poems in each category tell the story. The two poems of decay speak of my deepest doggerel days of disillusionment – times when my self-alienated feelings were at zenith. Such stages are necessary within what we might conceive as 'alchemical transmutation' of our life, on the most meaningful level. Well those two poems reflected me in both a milder and more extreme form.

The path into re-emergence, for me, came in two different forms of collaborative work. The first poem was co-written by myself and a gentleman on a project, where we each wrote a line and then the other developed the story in response to the last offered line. It was interesting to see how that morphed in creative tandem, into a powerful story – one which we all should be able to relate to. Carrying potential seeds of despair, it also offered the beacon of hope through a dialogue, reflecting the ups and downs of our human journey (my contributions to that piece in **bold**). The final poem also a collaboration, started with me setting the scene of a story with a group by writing the first five lines to a tale and then respondents added in characters. There was a musical component (percussion to augment voice) and these ideas were then incorporated into a poem by myself with a simple tune, carrying elements in style of a 'nonsense poem' - again the breaking down of classical forms. The result was a melody conducive to the style of soul and the deep south. For me, it reflected most of all that creativity (at its best) has a community dimension that leads to participation and response – a space in which we can create our own shared meanings, rather than having to swallow the prescriptions prefabricated for us in our formal straitjackets. That piece seemed like the fitting point at which to sign off, with a constructive vision of poetic and storied creations which can inspire us as communities, above any individual experience we may these days usually incline toward.

<u>Decay</u>

Mirage of Hope

How deep the pit, the seemingly bottomless void?
From whence I dredge endless slurry for gold; fool's gold
Someone shone a light called 'hope'
Or was it a beast juggling a near flat-battery torch?
Flicker, flicker

It's darkest just before the dawn, they say
Well, the next false dawn's never far away
When will the torturers bring their bitter embrace?
Once I see the would-be angel's face?

No sword cuts like that of familiarity
There's nowhere called "rock bottom"
When you're on the slippery slope to oblivion
Everything breaks down
And finally, so do I…

Nemesis

What is that thing, darting between the murky shadows?
It creeps around, a half-life in drag
It says, feebly at first…
and then with belly full of fire
"Someone, I used to be someone"
"Now I'm just some THING
 some fucking abomination"
The waste product that even a devil…
would contentedly flush away
"Yes, yes, I used to be someone…
 of that I'm pretty damned sure"
What the hell will come of me…
 should I fail to find a cure?
I've tried all of those shadows on for size
Each and every one of them, I now utterly despise
Maybe I should preach to you
And skillfully cajole?
But that would be a distraction to escaping from this hole
What *is* that thing, darting between the familiar shadows?
That creeps around,
 a prisoner of the night
A chill wind greets it at every street corner
No manner of clothing
 able to keep its piercing at bay.
Each and every door remains locked
Alas only silence, the eternal companion, looks on
Periodically arrives the season…
 of forlorn hope…
That even a single street light,
Should offer some dim hue

"Solace, solace" I hear you say?
That will prove impossible,
 unless one desists from the play
Maybe it's academic,
 a karmic fait accompli?
Or just maybe, the suffering ends…
 when I'm content just being me.

Re-emergence

Punch Drunk

Drinking life large through the straw of life
Living every day on the edge of a knife
Dodging looming pitfalls of a life of strife
But through all of these, I knew I was right.
I'm nearing the end, twelfth round of the fight.
Punch drunk, then rallying, we're getting there alright
I stagger, I stall, I tumble, I fall
No, really, I'm winning – corner, don't throw in the towel
It's all history now, giving way to the post-match brawl
It was a good fight Jerry, but I'd say most of all
"This mad hype machine it's mean, it's lean, it's keen"
And after tonight's performance, what does it all mean?
"Pack it, sack it, jack it, cos I'll never crack it"
"Come on Jerry, there wasn't so much in it"
"Call me a cynic lad, but I'm in it to win it"
"Surely the match fee you've received should do it?"
All questions no answers: that's life in the fast lane.
Please come back next time and we'll do it all again
…and again
…and again
…and

Down to the River

I woke up this morning
Got out of my bed
The Sun it was shining
So when I was fed
I went down to the river
Walked past a bush
In the bush there was a bird
It was a song thrush
It sang me a song
So I sang right along
Next I spied a dog
And very, very soon
It danced to my tune

Further on I met a cat
And the cat it wore a hat
I smiled at the cat
And it smiled right back
Then I saw a goat
It was up on a hill
It was eating its fill
It skipped over the ground
And walked with me to town
Then we walked right back
Along our dusty track
Then under a long bridge
We saw a pale white ghost

And the ghost said "Boo"
So what did we do?

Printed in Poland
by Amazon Fulfillment
Poland Sp. z o.o., Wrocław